CW00731562

Going to the Zoo

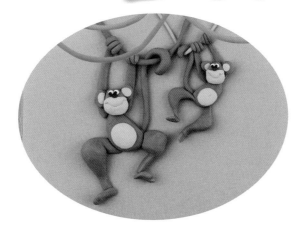

Written by Reece Cox

Illustrated by Luciana Fernandez

Collins

I'm going on a trip to the zoo,
If you want, you can come too.
Fasten your seatbelt in the car,
It won't take long, it's not very far.

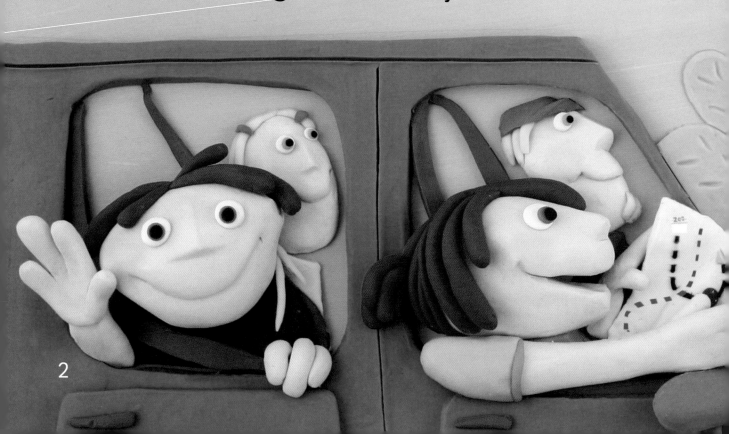

3

The parrots are eating carrots,
Monkeys have huge knees,
Giraffes like to laugh and sing,
And chimpanzees eat peas!

Penguins skiing on the water,
Elephants drinking tea,
Tigers munching crunchy crisps,
Kangaroos tickling me!

Crocodiles like giving smiles,
And stripy zebras too.

Bears like to hide in their lairs,
And lions love to shout BOO!

We've finished looking round,
so let's have a drink.
It's a very funny zoo, tell me,
what do you think?

12

13

My trip to the zoo

CAFÉ

15

Ideas for reading

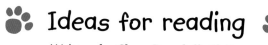

Written by Clare Dowdall, PhD
Lecturer and Primary Literacy Consultant

Reading objectives:
- be encouraged to link what they read or hear read to their own experiences
- discuss the significance of the title and events
- learn to appreciate rhymes and poems
- apply phonic knowledge and skills as the route to decode words

Spoken language objectives:
- listen and respond appropriately to adults and their peers
- select and use appropriate registers for effective communication
- use relevant strategies to build their vocabulary
- maintain attention and participate actively in collaborative conversations
- give well-structured descriptions, explanations and narratives for different purposes

Curriculum links: Citizenship; Art and Design

High frequency words: I'm, on, a, to, the, if, you, want, can, too, your, in, it, take, very, not, are, have, like, and, water, me, their, love, so, very, what, do

Interest words: zoo, fasten, seatbelt, parrots, monkeys, giraffes, chimpanzees, penguins, skiing, elephants, tigers, kangaroos, crocodiles, zebras, bears, lions

Resources: collage materials, pens and paper, animal name flashcards, ICT

Word count: 105

Build a context for reading

- Ask children if they have been to a zoo and challenge them to name zoo animals.

- Explain that this book is a poem, and that it might have rhythm and a rhyming pattern, which can help with reading.

- Read the title and blurb aloud together. Help children to read with expression, emphasising the title and the rhyming pattern.

- Show children the flashcards. Help them read the names using phonics and other strategies, e.g. familiar parts of words – *pen-guins*.

Understand and apply reading strategies

- Model how to read pp2–3 aloud, using expression and the rhyming pattern for effect.

- Read pp4–5 aloud together, looking at the pictures of the creatures described.